www.CreativeVoyagers.com

Dedicated to everyone who has stopped to gaze at the clouds.

Published in Denver, USA and Wellington, New Zealand by Creative Voyagers.

The author and illustrator would like to thank
Natasha Hanson and Shane Rempala for their invaluable assistance.

ISBN 978-0-9838019-0-0

www.CreativeVoyagers.com

THE WHENS

Steve Hanson
illustrated by *Louisa Rempala*

I was walking down the trail of Whens
a great distance from where I started.

A great house..

Like most people, I knew I would be happy when....
when I became rich...
when I looked perfect...
when I was a famous writer...

I visited a lot of those Whens, but I never stayed very long.
I could always see a bigger, better When on the edge of the
hazy blue horizon.

One day, while standing by an impressive When, I tried
something I had never done before - I looked behind me.
In the distance, I saw the young woman hoping to get to my
impressive When and the man behind her dying to get to her
When. Their bodies creaked with worries. They weren't happy.

I also realized I was not happy.

Shocked by my realization, I stood awkwardly by my current When. He was a pleasant chap about the size of a mini-refrigerator with blue fur as thick as a brazil shrub. He had orange teeth and smelled of golden honey.

But he wasn't magical. He couldn't make me happy.
He couldn't change my mood. He just pointed to the next
bigger, better When on the edge of the hazy blue horizon.
All he could do was point.

So I stepped off the well-beaten path to sit under a birch tree.
I had a great view of the trail of Whens
and an even better view of the clouds.

go back
on the path

You never forget your first cloud.
Mine was a cross between a tyrannosaurus
and a wooden stool but much softer and
gentler.

Over the next couple of months,
I carefully watched the trail of Whens and the clouds.

perfect grades

The fastest man on the trail passed four people but he never stopped to look at the clouds. He missed an ethereal lollipop castle-cloud when he was getting good grades.

He missed a three-legged frog-cloud when he was getting into a good law school and a glittering diamond forest when he was getting a good internship. I cried wondering what he will miss when he becomes a firm partner.

I was so moved by the clouds.
I began to write about every cloud I had ever seen and for the first time I smiled. I wrote and smiled and wrote until the grass grew higher than my shoulders.

A soft rustle of the wind caught my ear
and I put my pencil down.
What would I do on a cloudless day?
What if I ran out of birch bark to write on?
What if I never won an award?
Where would I find readers?

I knew I needed some readers to be a writer.
I packed up my birch bark to head towards the hazy
gray horizon where I saw a small group of readers.
I was sure I would be happy when I heard them gasp
at the beauty of my cloud descriptions.

That's when I fell to the ground laughing. All those worries were the soft rustling of the Whens trying to lure me back onto their trail. I had almost been fooled into thinking I could find happiness outside of myself.

I have spent all my days under the birch tree.
I have not sold many books or even won an award
(although my depiction of a buffalo horned cactus-cloud
is breathtaking).

I write because it makes me happy
and I am happy now because I write.
But most importantly I smile all the time.

My Whens know I only listen to my smile and that I will never return to their trail. So one by one, they can leave to do what they have always wanted. The end.

www.ingramcontent.com/pod-product-compliance
Lightning Source LLC
Chambersburg PA
CBHW041557120626
46551CB00002B/236